williambee

Published by
PEACHTREE PUBLISHERS
1700 Chattahoochee Avenue
Atlanta, Georgia 30318-2112
www.peachtree-online.com

First published in Great Britain in 2017 by Jonathan Cape,
an imprint of Random House Children's Publishers UK
First United States version published in 2016 by Peachtree Publishers

The illustrations were rendered digitally.

Printed and bound in November 2015 by Leo Paper Products in China

10 9 8 7 6 5 4 3 2 1 (hardcover)
10 9 8 7 6 5 4 3 2 1 (trade paperback)
First edition

Cataloging-in-Publication Data is available from the Library of Congress.

ISBN 978-1-56145-867-7 (hardcover)
ISBN 978-1-56145-946-9 (trade paperback)

1
2
3
4
5
6
7

To:
From:

AIR MAIL

1st

3rd

DO NOT BEND!

williambee
Stanley
the Mailman

PEACHTREE
ATLANTA

It's still dark outside, but the lights are on in Stanley's Post Office.

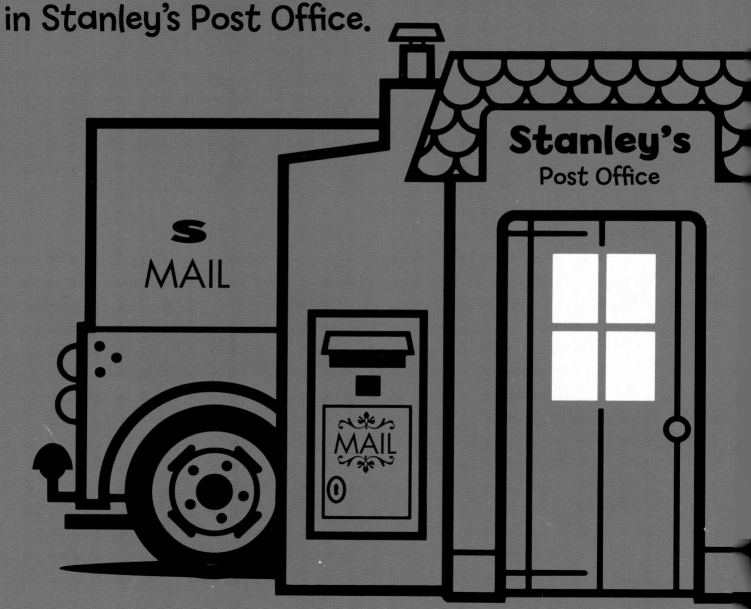

Stanley gets up very early to sort all the packages and letters.

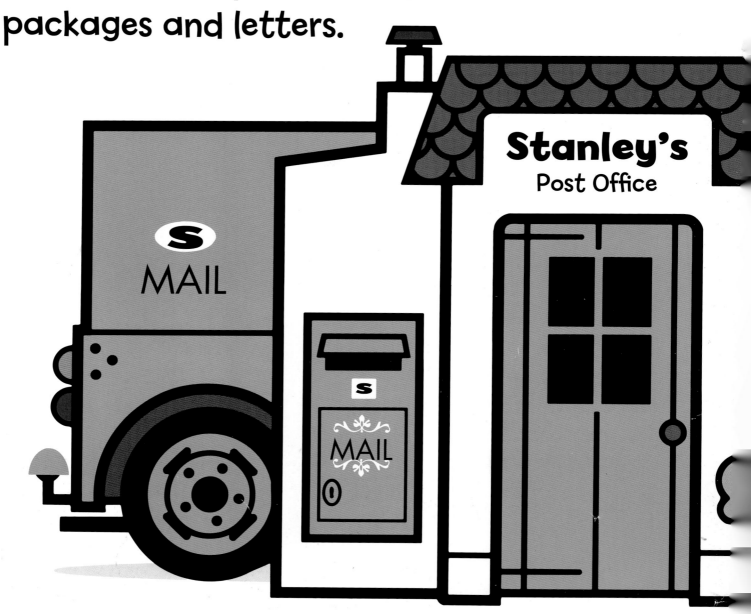

Then he sets off on his scooter.
Everyone will be waiting for their mail!

The first stop is Myrtle's house.
Myrtle is delighted—it's something she ordered
from her favorite fancy shop in Paris.

Myrtle's
House

What a lovely big box!
What a lot of tissue!

What a tiny little hat.

Next Stanley stops at Shamus and Little Woo's house. It's a present for Little Woo. He's very excited!

The present is from
Grandma and Grandpa.

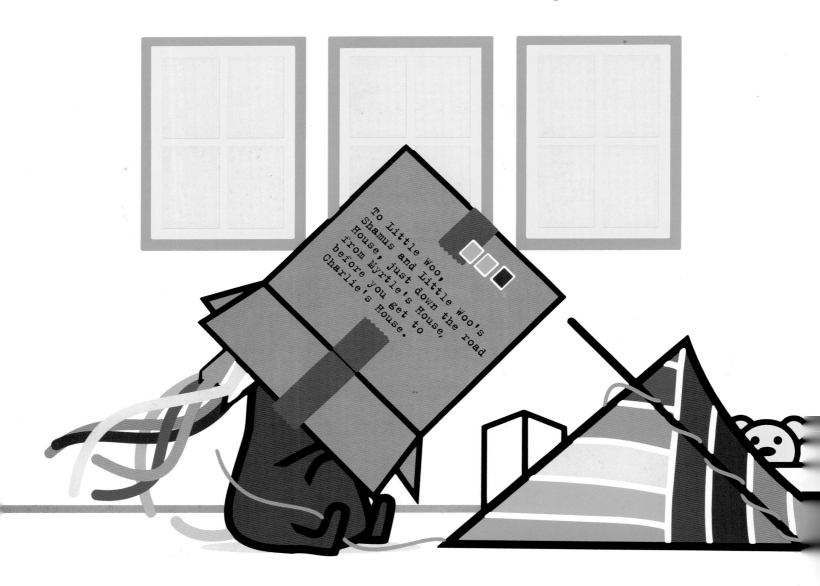

But what is it?
Luckily Little Woo's dad knows.

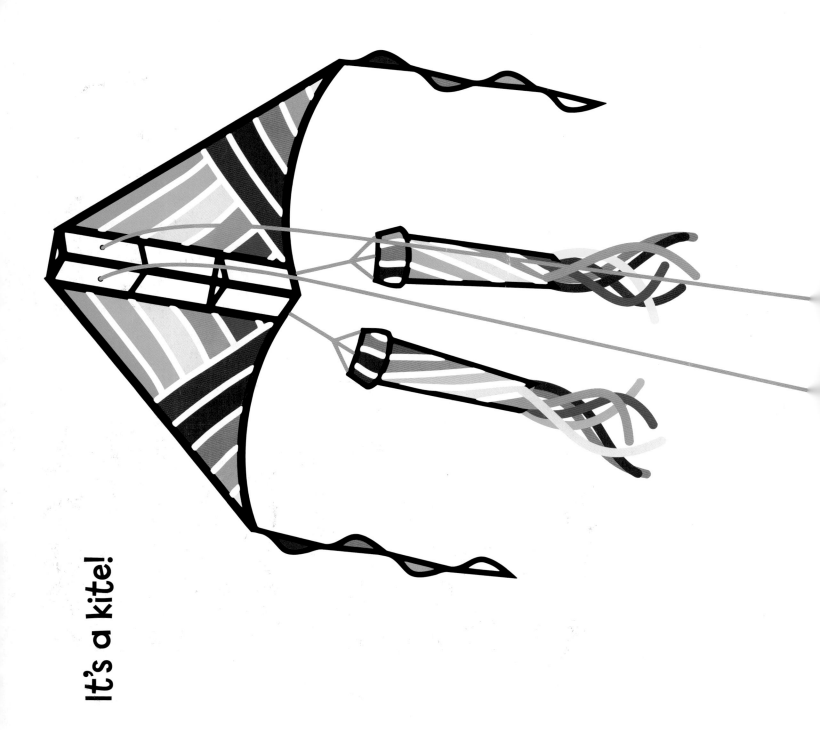

It's a kite!

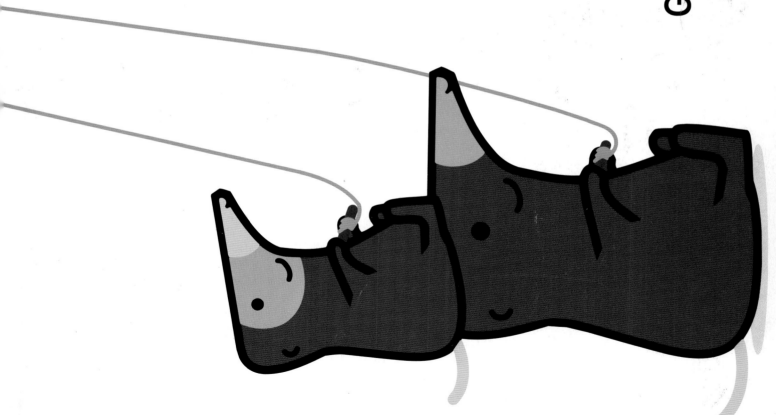

Thank you, Grandma! Thank you, Grandpa!

The next stop is Charlie's house. Charlie has so much mail that Stanley has gone back to the post office to get his van.

Charlie gets a lot of love letters.

He's quite a catch!

But not everyone is happy with what they get. Hattie has another speeding ticket.
Thanks a lot, Stanley.

Hattie's
House

Well! What a busy day!

Time for supper!
Time for a bath!

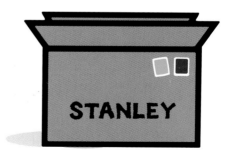

And time for bed!
Goodnight, Stanley.

Stanley

If you liked **Stanley the Mailman** then you'll love these other books about Stanley:

Stanley the Builder **Stanley's Garage**

Stanley's Diner **Stanley's Store**

Stanley the Farmer

williambee